# The Picky Little WITCH

# The Picky Little WITCH

Written by Elizabeth Brokamp
Illustrated by Marsha Riti

SPIT of BUG

WIZARD'S SNEEZE

TOENAIL of BAT

EYE of NEWT

PELICAN PUBLISHING COMPANY

GRETNA 2011

*For Lukas, Noelle, and Zoe - EB*

*The word "Pelican" and the depiction of a pelican are
trademarks of Pelican Publishing Company, Inc., and are
registered in the U.S. Patent and Trademark Office.*

**Library of Congress Cataloging-in-Publication Data**

Brokamp, Elizabeth.
  The picky little witch / by Elizabeth Brokamp ; illustrated by Marsha Riti.
    p. cm.
  Summary: Mama Witch tries to get her daughter to eat some Halloween soup before going out to
trick-or-treat, but Picky Little Witch finds many reasons to refuse. Includes a recipe for soup.
  ISBN 978-1-58980-882-9 (hardcover : alk. paper)  [1. Food habits—Fiction. 2. Witches—
Fiction. 3. Halloween—Fiction.]  I. Riti, Marsha, ill. II. Title.

PZ7.B7863Pi 2011
  [E]—dc22

                              2011004655

Printed in Singapore
Published by Pelican Publishing Company, Inc.
1000 Burmaster Street, Gretna, Louisiana 70053

# The Picky Little Witch

Mama Witch was very excited about the surprise treat she was making for Little Witch for Halloween. The big, black cauldron hissed and bubbled, releasing hot spray into the air, while Mama Witch looked proudly at her creation.

"What better thing is there to eat
than Halloween Soup for trick-or-treat?
For inside this tasty witch's stew
Are yummy things brewed just for you."

"What's in there?" asked the Picky Little Witch, peering at the greenish-brown liquid and wrinkling up her nose.

"Eye of newt, toe of sock, heel of boot, salted rock, Hair of slug, wart of frog, spit of bug, and mold on log."

Mama Witch stirred the pot with a gnarled tree branch, pausing to perform a taste-test. "MMMmmmmm," she said, licking the end of the stick clean. "Yum!"

"Yuck," said the Picky Little Witch.

"Eyelash of snake, toenail of bat, a tummy's ache, and wings of gnat,
Cough of spider, elbow of ghost, balls of fire, and burned-up toast."

"Gross," said the
Picky Little Witch.

"Pinch of snail, shower of soil, clippings of tail, dropper of oil,
Goblin tears and gremlin knees, vampire ears, and wizard's sneeze."

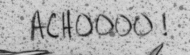

ACHOOOO!

"And a pinch of salt and pepper for seasoning," Mama Witch added.

"Barf," said the Picky Little Witch.

"Snout of anteater? Scream of wheat? Surely there's something here you'll eat."

But no matter what Mama Witch mentioned, the Picky Little Witch shook her head.

"How are you ever going to grow big and scary?" Mama Witch asked.

The Picky Little Witch shrugged her shoulders. An exasperated Mama Witch ladled out a bowl of soup and held it out to her daughter. "Try it," she said.

"I can't," said the Picky Little Witch. "I might throw up."
"That's okay," said Mama Witch. "A cleaning spell
will take care of the mess."

"I think I'm allergic to goblin tears. I'm almost positive," the Picky Little Witch said.

"Really? What happens?" Mama Witch asked.

"Well, I'm pretty sure that smoke comes out of my ears, my face swells up, and I can't talk."

"Hmmm," said Mama Witch. "That's terrible. We'll have to take you to the witch doctor right away. You'll miss trick-or-treating."

"Well, maybe it's not an allergy, exactly. It's more like a very sudden sickness that goes away really fast, as long as I get far, far away from the soup. Oh, no!" she said, running to the mirror. "Look at me. I'm turning green!" the Picky Little Witch gasped, peering at her reflection in the mirror.

"You're always green," her mama said. "Try the soup."

The Picky Little Witch took the bowl. She looked at her mama. Her mama pointed at the bowl.

Holding her nose with one hand and a spoon with the other, the Picky Little Witch took a deep breath and slurped the soup.

"Well?" said Mama Witch, expectantly.

"It's o-kaaaay," the Picky Little Witch said, taking another spoonful. "I mean, for something I *have* to eat. I don't think it will kill me or anything," she said, taking the bowl in her hands and noisily drinking up all the soup. She scraped up the last bit with her spoon, licked her lips, and even let out a little burp.

Burp!

"Ex-cu-use me!" the Picky Little Witch sang out, covering her mouth and giggling.

"'Burp of witch' wasn't one of the ingredients!" Mama Witch said, trying not to smile.

"Now can we trick-or-treat?" she asked her mother.
"Grab your broom. More tricks than treats, I hope,"
said Mama Witch.
"No way!" said the Picky Little Witch, heading out
the door.

"What better thing is there to eat
on Halloween night than a treat?
Go door-to-door and just say 'Boo!'
And they'll throw yummy treats at you."

"Candy apples on a stick,
lollipops to lick, lick, lick,
chocolate bars, rice crispy squares,
marshmallow stars, cream-filled éclairs."

"Too sugary," said Mama Witch, watching
as the Picky Little Witch collected goodies.

"Lemon drops, cookie crumbles,
ice-cream pops, and sprinkle-tumbles,
butterscotch sticks, coconut cakes,
jello mix, and licorice snakes," the Picky Little
Witch said, licking her lips.

"Much too human," said Mama Witch.

She and Picky Little Witch stopped in front of another house.

"Blueberry pie and gummi bears,
the funnel cakes found at fairs,
butter toffee, caramel dandy,
coffee milkshakes, cotton candy . . ." the Picky Little Witch said, dreamily.

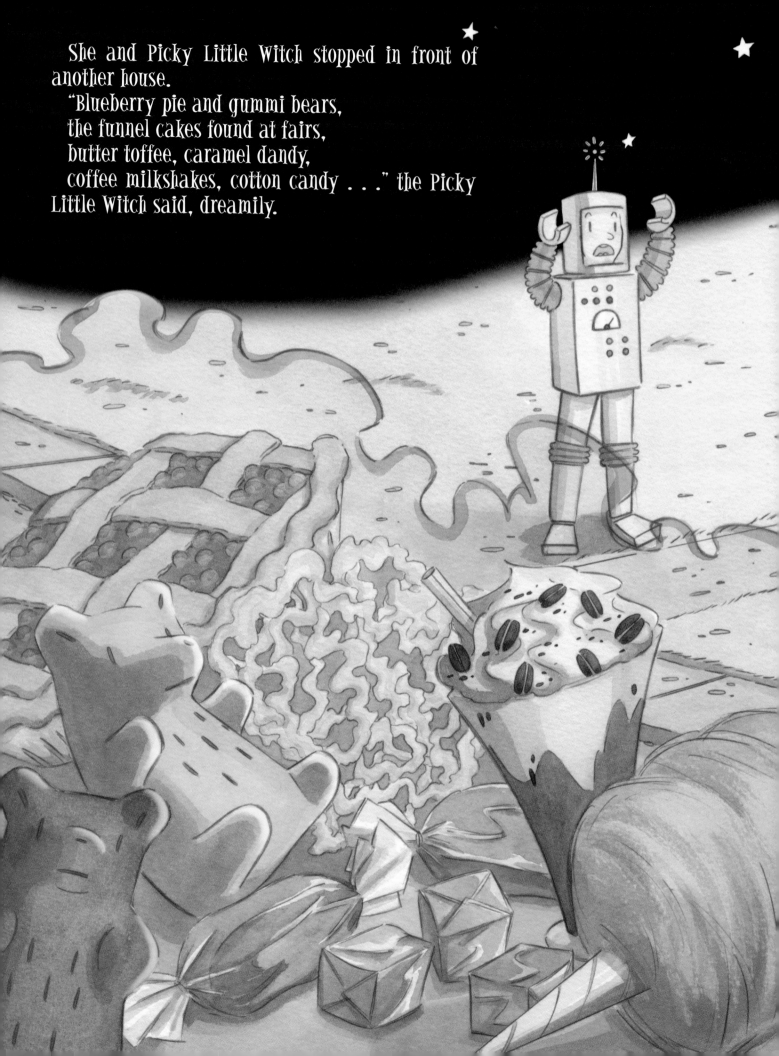

"Blech," Mama Witch said, shuddering.

"Try some, Mama," the Picky Little Witch said,
holding out her bag of treats.
"Oh, I couldn't eat another thing," Mama Witch said.
"I'll burst."
"I can do a cleaning spell and clean up all your
pieces," Picky Little Witch said.

"Well, I probably wouldn't really burst, exactly," Mama Witch said. "But it might make me too sweet. Witches can't be sweet, you know."

"Oh, Mama. That's silly! Try some," said the Picky Little Witch, holding out a chocolate bar.

"Maybe I'm allergic?" Mama Witch said, hopefully.

The Picky Little Witch shook her head.

Mama Witch sighed, unwrapped the shiny silver foil, and took a little nibble, then another, and another.

"Well?" asked the Picky Little Witch.

"Mmm, not *so* terrible," said Mama Witch, gobbling up the rest of the bar, and then licking the sticky sweetness off her fingers one by one. "I mean, I don't feel like I'm going to keel over or anything."

The Picky Little Witch raised her eyebrows.

"Actually, I kind of like it," Mama Witch whispered. "But don't tell anyone."

"I kind of liked your soup, too," the Picky Little Witch whispered back.

Mama Witch checked herself in the mirror. Still green. Still big. Still scary. "Phew!"

Picky Little Witch checked out her own reflection. Still green. Still cute. Still scary. "Phew!"

She and her mama looked at each other and smiled.
Maybe trying new things wasn't so frightening after all.

# Halloween Soup

Want to make your own Halloween soup? Because "eye of newt" and Mama Witch's other ingredients are hard for mere mortals to come by, we've made some substitutions. Cook up this recipe for a scrumptious green Halloween soup, guaranteed to fill your tummy with steamy goodness. Best when served followed by a fun night of trick-or-treating!

*Recipe courtesy of food educator and counselor Mary Porter.*

2 tablespoons vegetable oil
1 large onion, diced
2 large ribs celery, sliced
2 large carrots, peeled and sliced
1 large russet potato, peeled and diced
6 cups low-sodium vegetable broth
3-4 cups chopped, mixed vegetables (broccoli, cauliflower, peas, and zucchini)
1 teaspoon salt
Pinch of ground white pepper

In a large saucepan, heat the oil over medium heat. Add onion and sauté until they begin to soften, about 3-5 minutes. Add celery and carrots and sauté 5 more minutes until soft. Add diced potato and stir. Let simmer for 2-3 minutes. Add vegetable broth and—while the soup is coming to a boil—add your mixed vegetables. After bringing soup to a boil, turn down heat and let simmer 30 minutes. Add salt and pepper. Puree soup using a blender or food processor. Thin with water or additional broth if desired and adjust seasonings. Makes 6-10 servings. Serve hot!